ADDIE'S BAD DAY

by Joan Robins • Pictures by Sue Truesdell

HarperCollins*Publishers*

I Can Read Book is a registered trademark of HarperCollins Publishers.

Addie's Bad Day
Text copyright © 1993 by Joan Robins
Illustrations copyright © 1993 by Susan G. Truesdell
Printed in the U.S.A. All rights reserved.
2   3   4   5   6   7   8   9   10
❖

Library of Congress Cataloging-in-Publication Data
Robins, Joan.
Addie's bad day / by Joan Robins ; pictures by Sue Truesdell.
      p.   cm. — (An I can read book)
Summary: When Addie gets a haircut she hates, she is too embarrassed to
come to her friend Max's birthday party.
ISBN 0-06-021297-7. — ISBN 0-06-021298-5 (lib. bdg.)
[1. Haircutting—Fiction.   2. Beauty, Personal—Fiction.
3. Friendship—Fiction.]   I. Truesdell, Sue, ill.   II. Title.   III. Series.
PZ7.R5555Af   1993
                                                                          92-13101
[E]—dc20
                                                                          CIP
                                                                          AC

to Connie

Addie peeked around the tree.
She did not see anyone.

"I will be right back, Mom,"

she called,

and she ran next door

to Max's house.

Addie pulled her hat down.

Then she peeked in the window.

"RUFF, RUFF," barked Ginger,

Max's dog.

The door opened.

"It's me," said Addie.

"Happy birthday, Max."

"I knew it was you," said Max.

"Come in, Addie."

7

"I will only stay a minute,"

said Addie.

"Here is your birthday card,

and here is your present."

"Thank you," said Max.

"You are early for the party,

but you can stay."

"No, I can't stay," said Addie.

"Why not?" asked Max.

"It is a bad day," said Addie.

"Read your birthday card,

and you will see why."

9

Max opened the card
and read:

HAPPY BIRTHDAY, MAX.

THE LEAVES FALL HERE.

THE LEAVES FALL THERE.

THE TREE IS BARE.

POOR TREE.

POOR ME.

I CANNOT COME TO YOUR

BIRTHDAY PARTY.

LOVE, ADDIE.

"But Addie, *why* can't you come

to my party?" asked Max.

"Your card does not say *why*."

"I can't take off my hat,"

said Addie.

"That is why."

"That is silly," said Max.

"It is not silly," said Addie.

"I hope you and Ginger

have fun without me.

I hope you have chocolate cake

with roses on top. . . .

Oh, this is a BAD day!"

"What happened?" asked Max.

"Tell me!"

"This morning," said Addie,

"my father took me for a haircut.

14

The barber put a big sheet

around me.

She wet my hair.

I shut my eyes.

She went *snip, snip, snip* . . .

15

"*snip, snip snip.*

Then she put a towel

over my head.

16

I opened my eyes . . . and

ALL my hair was on the floor!"

Addie began to cry.

"It is silly to cry," said Max.

"Your hair will grow back."

"Not in time for the party,"

said Addie.

"I look funny.

Everyone will laugh at me."

"Let me see," said Max.

"Not here," said Addie.

"Someone else might see me."

"Come into my room," said Max.

19

Addie sat down

on Max's tiger rug.

She put her hands over her eyes.

"Okay," she said.

"You can take my hat off now."

Max pulled off Addie's hat.

"ZOW-WEE!" he cried.

"Zow-wee *what*?" asked Addie.

"Your hair is growing back!"
said Max.

"Come look in the mirror."

22

Addie peeked into the mirror.

"See?" said Max.

"You have more hair than I do.

So you *can* come

to my birthday party."

"No I can't!" said Addie.

"I look like an ugly-wugly."

"Then I," said Max, "look like

a . . . pugly-mugly."

"An *ugly* pugly-mugly!" said Addie.

She grabbed her hat from Max

and put it on.

"RUFF, RUFF," barked Ginger.

"Poor Ginger.

We left her all alone,"

said Max.

Addie and Max ran to find Ginger.

"Oh NO!" cried Addie.

"Ginger is chewing up your present.

What a BAD DAY this is!"

"It is NOT!" yelled Max.

"It's my birthday!"

He grabbed the box from Ginger.

"WOW, Addie, you got me a
jungle suit!

I will wear it to my party."

"I have one just like it,"
said Addie.

"Wear it to my party," said Max.

"That's it!" said Addie.

"We can be the jungle twins,

Ugly-Wugly and Pugly-Mugly.

No one will be able

to tell us apart!"

Addie ran out the door.

"Hurry back, Ugly-Wugly,"

yelled Max.

"See you soon, Pugly-Mugly,"

yelled Addie.

"RUFF, RUFF," barked Ginger.